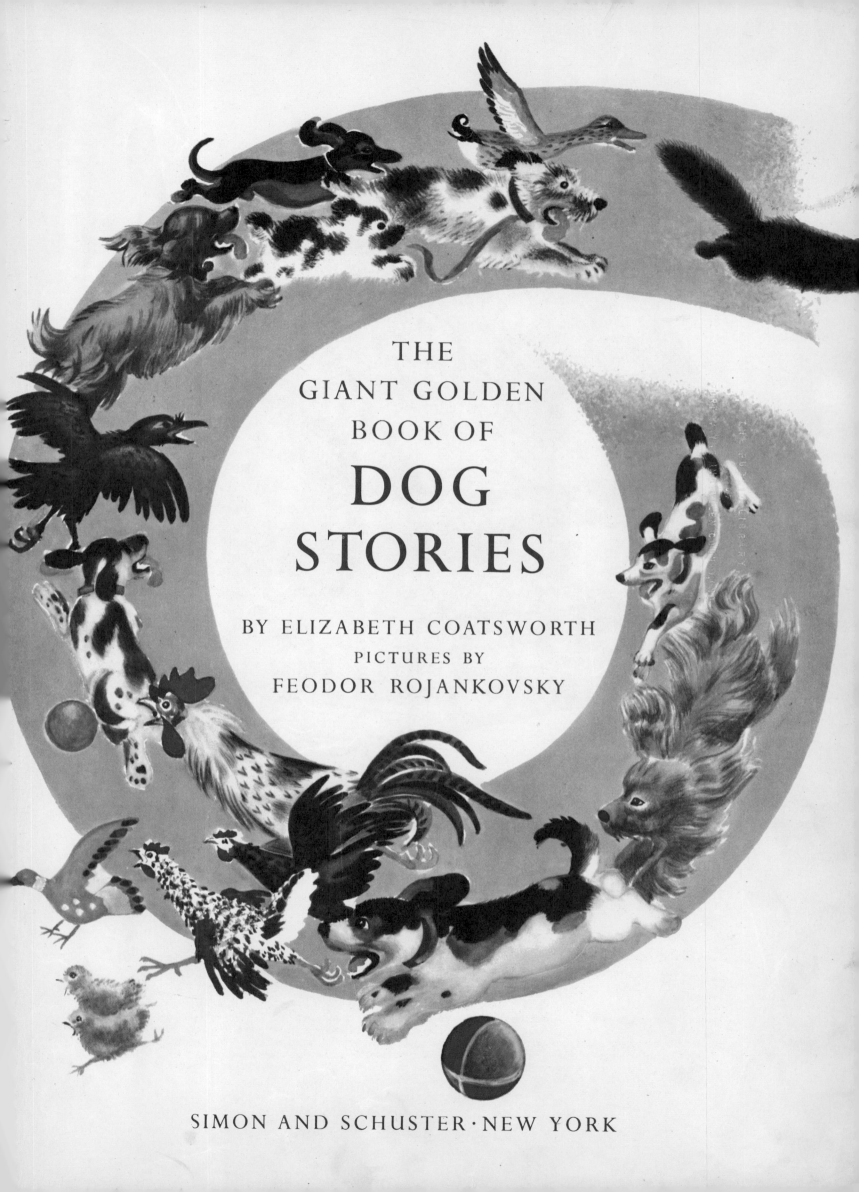

THE GIANT GOLDEN BOOK OF DOG STORIES

BY ELIZABETH COATSWORTH
PICTURES BY
FEODOR ROJANKOVSKY

SIMON AND SCHUSTER · NEW YORK

WITH LOVE
TO HELEN AND IVAN HEKIMIAN

The author and publishers thank the *Christian Science Monitor* for the following stories which appeared in that publication: "The Invisible Dog," "Eliza and the Hearth Rugs," and "Pug Island," copyright 1938, 1941, 1942, respectively, by Christian Science Publishing Society; copyrights assigned to Simon and Schuster, Inc., and Artists and Writers Guild, Inc.

Contents

POOR PENNY

PENNY, the cocker spaniel puppy, was happy all the afternoon. He had never had so much attention. Here were a little boy named John and a little girl named Eleanor who were willing to spend every minute playing with him. Here was a woman named Mummy who let him fall asleep on her lap when he felt tired. And here was a big man named Daddy who called him a handsome little fellow and made a snug box for him filled with fresh hay where he could sleep behind the kitchen stove.

Penny's brown eyes shone and his short tufted tail wagged all afternoon.

"Here, Penny! Here, Penny!" All the attention was for Penny, and at suppertime all the food was his. There weren't a lot of little brothers and sisters crowding around the dish, with their pink mouths going at full speed.

No, Penny was king in this new house. Everything was for Penny. He didn't miss his old home and his gentle long-eared mother, and his playful brothers and sisters. At least he didn't miss them much.

But after Penny had eaten his supper it began to grow dark. The lamps were lighted, but there were big shadows on the floor, and a cool little breeze moved under the doors, and the children grew tired of playing with Penny and asked their father to read out loud to them. But it was still all right, for their mother let Penny go to sleep again on her lap while she listened to the reading and darned socks. It was still all right with Penny.

But at last the mother looked at the clock and said, "Bedtime, children," and the children said it couldn't be so soon, but then they took Penny for a walk. He had never been out of the kennel-run at night before. The grass was wet with dew, and his fringed paws and the silky tips of his ears felt wet and heavy, and everywhere the shadows of trees looked like caves. But the children were with him. It wasn't too bad, though Penny skipped gladly enough back into the lighted house.

Then all the family trooped into the kitchen, and John lifted Penny into his bed, and patted him until he lay down.

"Good Penny! Good dog! Now go to sleep!"

"Good night, Penny!" said everyone, but the moment they started to go away, out jumped Penny, ready to follow.

John lifted him back. "Stay there, Penny. All of you go out of the kitchen, and then I'll run out and close the door."

But Penny could run faster than John could.

John put him back into his box, and this time he gave him a little slap on his shoulder. Penny looked at his new master with horror. What had Penny done? He was only showing that he loved John.

This time Penny waited a moment before he jumped, but even so he was at the door before John.

"He doesn't understand," said the father. "You'll have to put on his leash and tie him to the leg of the kitchen table. After we're gone, he'll get back into his box where it's nice and warm."

So Penny was tied and the light was put out and the door was closed and Penny was left alone in the dark.

Oh, then he missed his mother and his brothers and sisters! And he missed John and Eleanor and their father and mother. First he whimpered and then he howled. He pulled at his collar while his nails slid on the kitchen linoleum. He struggled and panted and then he howled again.

"Won't he ever go to sleep?" the children asked from the head of the stairs.

"After a while he'll see it doesn't do any good," their father answered, "and then he'll stop."

But an hour later Penny was still howling, whimpering, panting and scratching, and the children were on the stairs again.

"Please let me go in and pat him a little. He's so frightened," said John, starting down the stairs.

But Daddy called him back. "No. If he finds that making a fuss works, he'll do it every night," he said, looking harassed. "You children go to sleep."

"He's a great deal worse than any baby," said Mother. "Do you suppose this will go on all night?"

"Maybe, but we'll have to go to sleep. In a few days he'll stop."

"A few days?" echoed Eleanor. "Why, Daddy, it's dreadful. Penny's afraid."

"All new puppies have to get used to sleeping alone."

"But Penny's *afraid*. Couldn't I *please* put him at the foot of my bed?"

"Then he'd *never* learn to sleep by himself. No, after a few nights this will all be over. Back to bed with you both! Mummy and I are going to bed, too. Just pay no attention to Penny."

"But he sounds as if a wolf were after him."

"There isn't any wolf," said Daddy. "Now go to sleep."

But that wasn't easy with the desperate commotion in the kitchen. Sometimes everything would grow quiet. Then the wailing would begin again, louder than ever. But at last everyone except Penny did go to sleep.

Eleanor woke up sometime in the middle of the night. The house was in darkness, soft and kind as the velvet petals of a dark pansy, and she could see a few stars from where she lay. For a moment the only sound she heard was the steady ticking of the clock on her bureau. The clock was always company

for her when she woke up in the night, and in the morning it told her whether she could get up or whether she must lie in bed a little longer so as not to disturb other people.

Eleanor thought, "Penny's asleep, too. I'm glad."

But just then the whimpering began again. It was not so loud, but it seemed to Eleanor sadder than ever.

"Oh, dear! Oh, dear!" she thought. "There must be something I could do!"

The wailing died away.

"Tick, tock, tick, tock, tick, tock," remarked the steady clock in its sensible voice.

Eleanor crept out of bed. She had an idea. Tiptoeing over to her bureau, she felt for the clock; her hands closed upon it, round and comfortably fat. Down the stairs she went, one hand upon the banister. She felt her way down the hall and into the dining room. When she stumbled against the chair, Penny began to bark excitedly.

"Sh!" whispered Eleanor, "You'll wake up Daddy and Mummy."

For a moment she thought that she heard someone moving in the room above, but then there was silence again. In the kitchen, Penny was whimpering and panting, half choked as he struggled against the leash.

"Sh!" Eleanor said again, feeling her way along the sideboard to the swinging door.

As she pushed it open, there was a wild scrabble from Penny somewhere in the darkness. A moment later, she was kneeling beside him, and he was snuggling into her arms, lapping her face with joy.

Eleanor patted and patted the puppy until he was quiet. Then she put the clock on the floor not far from Penny's box.

"There, there, Penny," she whispered. "Tick, tock, tick, tock; the clock will take care of you, Penny dear."

She waited for a little while, kneeling beside Penny while they both listened to the clock. Then she crept away. Penny tried again to follow. There were a few howls. But even before Eleanor had reached the top of the stairs, the wailing had stopped. She went to bed and fell asleep in a silent house.

Eleanor woke up early to a sunshiny day. She could hear John in the shower and her father going downstairs.

When he saw her, he said, "Hello, Eleanor. You see the puppy quieted down all right. There hasn't been a peep out of him for hours."

Eleanor, still barefooted and in her nightgown, followed him to the kitchen.

There lay Penny fast asleep, curled up in a silken ball. But he was not in his box. No, he was on the linoleum with his head close to Eleanor's clock, which was saying in the steadiest way, "Tick, tock, tick, tock, tick, tock."

Her father gave the two a long look and then he looked at Eleanor.

"A very sensible idea," he remarked with a smile. And at his voice Penny woke up, eager for breakfast and a day of play.

THE INVISIBLE DOG

ONCE UPON A TIME there was a cat who came back from marketing one morning and heard a queer noise at the kitchen table. It was the sound of a fork touching against a china dish. She looked at the kitchen table and there, indeed, was a china dish heaped high with all the most delicious things from her cupboard and icebox, and there, too, was the fork moving busily to and fro from the dish to a certain place in the air. The fork left the dish loaded with a fine mouthful, and somewhere about a foot and a half above the plate the mouthful disappeared, but the astonished cat could see no mouth that was eating all these tidbits she had hoped to eat herself.

No paw was upon the fork, nothing seemed sitting on the chair drawn up to the table, and no one answered her when she cried out in a trembling voice:

"Who's eating my nice dinner?"

But still the fork went on busily emptying the plate and still there was the faint click of china and silver in the sunny kitchen.

The cat turned about, closed the kitchen door behind her, and holding the market basket still under her arm, hurried down the road to her neighbor's, the witch cat, whom she found stirring a queer-smelling pot on the fire, with her seven black daughters around her.

13

When the two cats arrived at the other house, they found the plate nearly empty, but the fork was still at work.

The witch cat crept silently towards the chair and then, standing on her tiptoes, suddenly emptied the herbs from the striped bag into the air as high as she could reach. There was an astonished yelp, and before their eyes appeared a spotted dog sitting on the chair, the fork clutched firmly in his greedy spotted paw.

"Wouldn't you have known it was a dog?" said Mrs. Miaou. "A dog! A horrid dog!"

The dog didn't look a bit ashamed. "I'd almost finished, anyway," he said, "and I was getting tired of being invisible. A fairy put the spell on me last week for digging up her flower garden, and I'm glad, ma'am, to have you take it off. Thank you both and good-by."

But the witch cat stood in front of the door.

"Oh, ma'am," said poor Mrs. Miaou, "the most curious thing is happening in my kitchen!"

And she told the witch cat and her seven daughters all about the mysterious fork that was eating up her dinner.

"Here," said the witch cat briskly to her daughters, "you stir the brew while I'm gone and, mind you, don't let it boil over! Mrs. Miaou, I'll be ready to go in less time than it takes to jump over a broomstick."

And quickly putting on her bonnet and shawl, she reached up to the shelf where she kept her magic herbs, and taking a pinch from this bowl and a pinch from that, she shook them into a striped paper bag, and turned to her visitor.

"Not so fast, my blithe young dog," she said. "You've eaten up Mrs. Miaou's good food and now you go out and pay for it by chopping up kindling for her for a couple of hours."

"Suppose I won't?" said the spotted dog.

"Then I'll sprinkle you with some more herbs and turn you into a sausage!" said the witch cat.

The spotted dog didn't like that idea at all, so he went out to the wood-pile and all afternoon he split wood. Mrs. Miaou praised his strength and dexterity, and he began to enjoy his work and whistled loudly. So Mrs. Miaou gave him his supper and they parted the best of friends, but the witch cat had gone home long ago to make sure that her seven black daughters didn't allow the brew to boil over.

I AM A BAD DOG

I am a bad dog,
A bad dog,
A bad dog.
I howl,
And I growl,
And I chew up people's shoes.
And when someone
Calls me,
Calls me,
Calls me,
I run
(Just for fun)
Right away, if I choose.

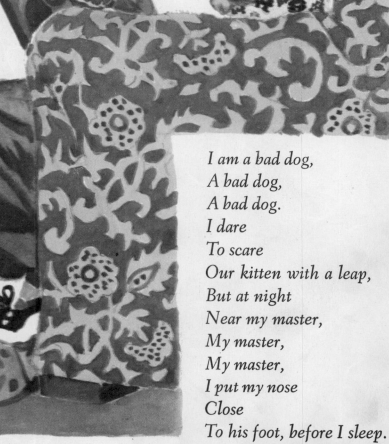

I am a bad dog,
A bad dog,
A bad dog.
I dare
To scare
Our kitten with a leap,
But at night
Near my master,
My master,
My master,
I put my nose
Close
To his foot, before I sleep.

PLEASE, MOTHER, PLEASE

I wanted a dog
And, Mother, see,
Here is a dog
Who's been wanting me!

He hasn't a collar,
He's dirty and thin,
Please, Mother, please,
Let me take him in!

See how he wags
His tail when I call,
And how ready he is
To play at ball!

TRAIN SOUNDS

ON CLEAR DAYS we hear the train whistle well enough, but on misty days it seems to sound just at the foot of our fields. Then the railroad cars seem to tread heavily across the pasture. Bump, bump, bump! they go and hoot, hoot, hoot! shrieks the engine, setting the dogs to barking. It puts one in mind of traveling. But where shall we go?

17

HE WILL BE YOUR FRIEND

Who will bring in the sheep?
The collie will.
He will bark, he will run
Until his work is done.
He will bring in the sheep.

Who will guard the house?
The watchdog will.
He will listen, he will wait,
No one shall pass the gate.
He will guard the house.

Who will be my friend?
The house dog will.
He will love you, he will stay
By your side, night and day.
He will be your friend.

THE OLD DOG

ANY YEARS AGO, before you were born but not before I was, an old dog guarded the sheep on the hills of Smyrna.

"What is a dog?" the shepherds said. "A dog is nothing. If a dog dies, one gets another dog. That is all."

But somehow this old dog was more than a dog. She was wise. She was brave. Day and night she guarded the sheep on the barren hills. She knew when a lamb was lost among the rocks and went to find it. She fought the wolves and drove them away from the flock.

"If the old dog is with us," the shepherds said, "a man may lie and watch the stars at night, with an easy heart. She will look after everything."

So great did this old dog's fame become, that other shepherds came to buy her puppies to take care of their sheep, hoping that they would be faithful, like the old dog. They actually paid for the puppies in money or in lambs. In that country, where dogs were not much regarded, this was a great thing.

Now one morning, when the little clouds of spring seemed like white sheep in a blue meadow, and the brooks were running over with water and the cress grew green in the current, the old dog seemed very uneasy. She ran now here, now there, looking and whining under her breath.

"What is wrong?" asked the two shepherds, and they counted the sheep.

"They are all here, Old Dog," they said. "Every lamb is beside its mother. Stop running and whining. Nothing is wrong."

But the old dog scarcely looked at the shepherds when they spoke to her.

Still she went about, whining under her breath, her eyes anxious.

"The old dog is foolish with age," said one shepherd.

"See!" exclaimed the other. "She is running off, away from us and the flock! Old Dog! Old Dog! Come back!"

But the old dog ran on, and though the shepherds shouted and shouted, they were soon left to guard the flock by themselves.

All day the shepherds watched the sheep without a dog to help them. How they had to run to head off the flock when it went too near the cliffs! How they had to search the little valleys to make sure that no lamb was left behind, out of sight among the rocks. That day there was no rest for them.

"After all these years, the old dog has become good-for-nothing like a common dog," they said angrily. "We shall have to find another dog which won't run off and leave us."

19

But as the dusk began to settle down over the hills and the coolness spread from the shadows, the old dog came back, and behind her there followed three of her sons and two of her daughters, full-grown dogs now, and each with his or her own flock somewhere to guard.

"But these dogs have all been sold!" cried the shepherds. "We have had money for them, or lambs. That dog with the lop ears belongs to a man ten miles to the east of us! And that one with the white face comes from seven miles to the west! They all come from far away, except the big one which belongs to our neighbor. The men who bought them will think that we have been whistling them back so that we may sell them again. What can we do?"

"We must drive them back to their masters," said one. "We shall be known as thieves. What a wicked old dog ours is to get us into this trouble!"

"She is indeed too old for her work," said the other. "Now she thinks only of having a good time, and invites all her family to visit her. We must teach her and them their duty again, it seems!"

And the shepherds began to throw stones at all the dogs.

But the dogs only ran beyond reach of the stones and sat down, their tongues hanging out. If the men ran towards them, they moved to the other side of the flock, but they would not leave. The old dog, too, for once would not let the shepherds come near her. She, like the young dogs, kept the flock between herself and her masters.

In Smyrna the darkness comes early, and soon the men could no longer see to chase the dogs. They fell over rocks and scratched themselves on brambles.

"Let us go back to our fire," they said. "In the morning, if they are not gone, we shall find a way to get rid of them."

It was a clear night of stars and a small moon and a lonely wind. About midnight the wolves came, not one wolf nor two nor even three wolves, but a whole pack of wolves, perhaps ten or eleven of them.

And the old dog and her sons and daughters fought the wolves. They fought them hour after hour. They fought them all together, they fought them singly, on this side of the flock and on that side. The shepherds, roused by the clamor, tried to help the dogs, but they could see almost nothing. By the time they reached one scene of the fighting, it had stopped there and

begun somewhere else, as a wolf or two stole up to the sheep from a new direction.

But the dogs were everywhere. Not a dog sought the protection of the men; not a dog turned from the battle; and just before the day came, the wolves stole back into the high hills, leaving three of their dead behind them.

In the light of dawn, the shepherds could see the old dog and her children. They were bleeding and worn out with fighting, but they looked well pleased, and as the sun rose, the young dogs shook themselves and limped off towards their own masters.

The old dog trotted up to the fire for her breakfast. She looked at the shepherds, ready to obey them again, to fetch in this sheep or that one, to scatter the flock or to bunch it together.

The shepherds fed her well.

"Old Dog," they asked, "how did you know that the wolves were coming last night? What bird by the spring told you? What grasshopper brought you the tidings? With only our help, you could have done nothing. Half the flock would have been dead by now and the rest scattered and a further prey to the wolves. But you went to the north and the south and the east and the west and gathered your children for battle. Really, you are as wise as Ulysses. And this battle of the wolves and the dogs deserves to be remembered like the siege of Troy, when the Greeks fought with the Trojans."

But while the shepherds praised the old dog, she found a soft piece of turf and lowered herself upon it, slowly, grumbling a little because she felt bruised and sore. And there in the sun she closed one eye, while from the other she glanced towards her flock, which she would guard so long as there was breath in her body.

HERON FLYING

I N THE LATE, late afternoon, when all the farm lay in the shadow of the hill, the two heron, flying far overhead, were still in the sunlight. And from their high lane under the clouds they saw hills which no one on the farm could see. And below the hills there were ponds and woodlands and roads on which the automobiles came and went, and near one house, there was a dog lying in the sun by the kitchen door.

All these the heron saw, flying in the sunlight over the shadowy farm.

SNOW'S FAMILY

When Dan Forester left his fishing and went into the Labrador interior for the winter trapping, Snow's puppies were only three months old. Dan took the rest of his team, but left Snow at the house.

"Now, Tom," he said to his son, "you take care of your mother while I'm gone. I've left firewood enough, I think, but maybe you'll need to bring in more. You know how to snare rabbits and birds. I've left the light gun. If anything goes wrong, you go right off and get Mrs. Hardy. Their cove's only three miles off, if you go over the ice, and she's had lots of experience with sickness and cuts and burns. And that reminds me, be everlastingly careful of fire. Don't ever let the stove get red-hot. I should be back by April at the latest but don't worry if I'm late. I may need a few good skins and stay on a piece. You got all this clear?"

"Yes, Dad."

"There's one thing more. These puppies of Snow's. Snow's a good dog, but these young ones of hers are half wolf. I've watched them drink and every last one of them laps like a dog instead of sucking up the water, like a wolf. So they favor Snow. But they'll take careful training. I don't know as you have the skill."

"I've watched you, Dad. I'll try."

"See what you can do. They're promising. But if you can't manage them, shoot them. We don't want any wild dogs around these parts. That's about all, I guess. Good luck, Son. Time to say good-by to your mother and be off."

With his father away somewhere in the nameless barren interior, there was a great deal for Tom Forester to do. The house lay in a narrow cove between two rocky headlands, like granite paws stretched out into the sea. It was unpainted and weather-beaten, with only the boathouse by the stony shore for company, and their nearest neighbors three miles away by sea. But Mrs. Forester and Tom had known nothing different. They were used to hard work and getting along without things, and they would rather have lived in Forester's Cove than in any other place around the world.

Tom knew just what had to be done and how to do it. The only thing he wasn't sure about was how to train Snow's puppies. Whenever, during the short days, he had a spare half hour he played with them, or took his work near them so that they might hear his voice and get very used to having him around. It was he who always fed them their ration of frozen fish as they grew older.

There were five of them—big, strong-looking puppies now, all gray-brown like their wolf father, except one which was white. As they grew to their full size, Tom went over the second-team harness, oiling and mending it, and looked to the sled. But what should he do next? Usually his father broke in one young dog at a time with the rest of the team knowing just what to do, and that made it easier. But Tom would have nothing but young dogs, except for Snow.

Tom began to watch Snow more carefully. If two young dogs began to fight, Snow jumped in and separated them with a snarl and a few good nips.

When they went hunting she led, and if a young dog tried to pass her, she taught him his place at once.

"All right, Snow," Tom said. "You teach your puppies how to be sled dogs. You know. Now you show them."

The puppies allowed themselves to be put in the harness, each fastened to traces of different lengths. Snow's were the longest. For the first time in her life she was the lead dog, and had the position of honor. When Tom gave the signal, she was off. But what was the trouble? The puppies weren't following properly. They were biting at their traces, and getting tangled up, and playing with each other.

Like a blizzard of angry whiteness Snow fell upon them. Snarl, snap, snarl! She straightened them out and taught them their manners. Who can say how she told them what she expected of them? But somehow she let them know and they understood.

By April they were a fully trained team, working together and proud of themselves. Many times they had taken Mrs. Forester, wrapped in furs, over the ice to call on Mrs. Hardy, while Tom ran behind, holding the handlebars, or jumped onto the runners to share the wild scamper. Once or twice they had even ventured as far as Seal Cove, ten miles away, a regular village since four families lived there, and a whole pack of dogs would rush out to quarrel with the newcomers and had to be driven off with Tom's long-lashed whip.

Then one afternoon as the days began to lengthen and the snow to melt and the ice to darken and honey-comb, there was a shout from up the valley, and it was Dan Forester returning home, with his sled laden with prime skins of fox and marten.

Tom and Snow kept the young dogs in order while the old team trotted in, and the Foresters met again after so many months of separation.

Of course that first day they only *began* to learn their new skill. But every day, Tom and Snow put them through their paces and each day things went a little more smoothly. The puppies grew taller and stronger than their mother. They were beautiful creatures, handsome as their father, but with the assured dog look in their eyes and a different way of carrying their tails. But big as they were and strong as they were, they never snarled nor snapped back at their mother when she rushed among them to punish a disobedient or clumsy son or daughter.

Dan ran an interested eye over Snow's family.

"They're as handsome a lot as I've ever seen, Son," he said. "How do they work out?"

"Oh, pretty well, Dad," Tom answered modestly.

"We'll try the two teams tomorrow on the ice. It will hold for another week or two."

That night it was long before Tom could sleep, he was so excited and happy at having his father safe at home again. And then he thought about the next day. Perhaps, with the other dogs near by, his team would turn unruly. Anything might happen. But at last Tom fell asleep.

In the morning his father harnessed the first team and Tom harnessed his. Snow seemed irritable and out of temper. Perhaps she was nervous, too. Mrs. Forester rode on her husband's sled. All the old team behaved perfectly, but Snow's family was on edge, upset at having the strangers so near them, unsure of themselves because Tom and Snow were unsure,

too, this morning. Two of the young dogs fought over their positions on the team, each claiming the place next to Snow, and this time they snarled back at their mother when she turned on them. Finally they were off to a ragged start, with the first team drawing smoothly ahead.

Then slowly Snow's children settled down. In front of them ran their white mother; behind them was Tom, whom they knew so well. Each was in his or her place; each knew what to do. Snow's messages seemed to flow from her without need of bark or growl, and Tom's orders were understood almost before they were given.

The team was running now as with one will. They were catching up with the older dogs, but this Champion, the leader of the other team, would not permit. He lengthened his stride and the others followed. The sleds flew along. No need for Dan and Tom to urge them on. The dogs were racing, the

experienced team against the inexperienced one, the old dogs against the young ones, Champion, who had always been the leader, against Snow and her children. Faster and faster they ran with their drivers running beside them and the old ice flying.

Now Snow was nose to nose with Champion. They were nearing Hardys' Cove. The family and their dogs had come down to the beach to watch them in. Snow seemed to be flying, and not one of her children ran with slack trace. Like a whirlwind they passed Champion and the others; like a breaker they drove in upon Hardys' Beach amid a wild barking of dogs.

Later when they were alone Dan Forester put his hand on Tom's shoulder.

"That's as fine a team of dogs as I ever saw," he said. "They're yours, Son. I wasn't sure you could do it, but you trained them, and trained them fine."

Tom reddened with pleasure, but catching Snow's eye, he grinned.

"I guess they're really Snow's team, Dad," he said. "It was she did the training. I only helped a little."

27

THE NEW MEMBER

ALL THE DOGS in town liked to go with the postman when he delivered the morning mail.

The first one to join him was a cocker spaniel.

"Hello, Danny," the postman said.

Danny wagged his stub of a golden tail, and with his long silky ears almost touching the ground, trotted along with the postman.

Half a block farther on, a dachshund joined them.

"Hi, Franz!"

The dog looked up, wagged his long tail, and went along with the postman and Danny.

It was Freckles, the retriever, who joined them next, coming out of a red brick house, on purpose to go along.

And then an Irish terrier ran up, with an air of having just happened to see them, although the postman and all the other dogs knew that he had been waiting by the curb for half an hour, at least.

They all trotted at the postman's heels, enjoying dog gossip as they went along. They liked to walk with him. They knew exactly where he was going.

Their own masters and mistresses they couldn't count on. A dog could never tell *where* he'd be taken or what other dogs he'd meet with, when he went out with his own people, but with the postman it was different. A dog knew what to expect.

This morning, however, a new dog joined them, a big handsome police dog.

"Hi, fellow," said the postman, for he didn't know the new dog's name yet.

The big police dog seemed not to notice that he had been spoken to, but he came along with the others.

He crowded against Freckles, and Freckles moved over to give him more room.

He stepped on Franz, and Franz let out a yip of surprise, though of course, he wasn't hurt. But somehow none of the dogs was having as much fun as usual. Then the new dog gave a hard wag of his tail across Mike's face, and Mike, who had a short temper, growled at him.

"Sh!" said the postman, looking over his shoulder at them. "No quarreling in the dog club!"

It was just at that moment that the big dog saw

the gray-and-white cat, such a little cat, going quietly about her business.

He let out a great roar and rushed towards her, his big mouth open and all his long teeth showing. The cat saw him coming and climbed a tree just in time.

"Come back here!" scolded the postman. "If you chase a cat again, you can't walk with us. We know how to behave. Bad dog! Bad dog!"

But the police dog only looked pleased with himself.

"I nearly had her!" his look seemed to say. "I'm cock of the walk, I am, and everyone has to look out for me!"

Nothing more happened during that morning's walk, but none of the other dogs had a good time. The new dog put on airs with them. He acted as though they were beneath his notice.

Next morning everything began as usual. First Danny, the cocker, joined the postman, then little bowlegged Franz, then good friendly Freckles, and then Mike, his red ears pricked and his whiskers bristling as usual. They made such a good club, all used to one another and their own way of doing things.

But there, around the corner, appeared the big, handsome stranger. The postman shook his head at him. "No more chasing cats," he said severely. "We had enough of that yesterday."

But the dog was as proud as ever. He didn't care what the rules of the club were. They had only stopped at three houses to deliver the mail when they met the little gray-and-white cat again. This time she was crossing the backyard, going towards the garage.

The police dog gave a most terrible roar and sprang after her. There were no trees near by for the little cat to climb, and the big dog was close on her heels. At full speed, like a gray-and-white streak, flat to the ground, the little cat ran for the open door of the garage.

"Here, you!" shouted the postman, beginning to run after the police dog, with all the club at his heels.

"Come back here!" shouted the postman again.

But everything was happening so fast that no one could reach the garage in time to save the poor little cat. From the building ahead of them came the sounds of struggle, a roar, and a scuffle.

"The poor little thing's dead!" said the postman, running on.

He had just reached the door when he was almost knocked over, as out rushed the big dog, as fast as when he had gone in. He was yipping as he ran, and there was a wild look in his eye, and on his back rode the little gray-and-white cat, holding on with all her claws except when she loosened a front paw to give her mount another long scratch. And every time the claws went in, the big dog's yipping rose louder.

The postman didn't laugh. He just stood there with the four dogs at his heels. And in a minute the little gray cat dropped off the big dog's back and calmly trotted back towards the garage.

"I guess she's got kittens," the postman said. "You leave cats alone, fellow."

This time the police dog was glad to be spoken to. He wagged his tail and put his head under the postman's hand, asking to be comforted.

"Good dog," said the postman, kindly rubbing his ears. "Now you behave yourself and be a good member of the club."

The police dog dropped back in his place with the others. But today, he didn't crowd anyone. He didn't step on anyone. He didn't wag his tail in anyone's face. And Danny and Franz and good-natured Freckles and Mike trotted along companionably at his side. And as they went off, following the postman to ring the next doorbell, the little gray-and-white cat appeared again at the garage door, with three little gray-and-white kittens.

For a moment she looked after the departing dog club, and then, turning her back on them, she began to wash the face of one of her kittens, as though nothing in the world had happened.

THE PUPPY'S BOAST

I'm not afraid
Of any old thing,
I'd bark at a mouse
In the wainscoting,
I'd bark at a cat
On the kitchen step,
And the dog next door,
That big old shep.
But I wouldn't bark
At the milkman's horse
Unless the gate
Were closed, of course!

GYPSY DOG

Bow wow
Whose dog art thou?
The gypsy's dog—
See, he's coming now!
That is his horse
And that is his van,
And there you can see
The gypsy man.

You stay at home,
And say bow-wow
By the picket gate
As you're doing now,
But I roam the roads
With a horse and van,
For I am the dog
Of the gypsy man!

ELIZA AND THE HEARTH RUGS

HERE WAS ONCE a little girl named
Eliza who lived with her grandmother
all alone in a little red house. She would
have been happy except for one thing:
when she sat by the hearth, looking into the fire, it
did seem to her that it would be nice to have a dog
on one side of her to wag his tail when she spoke
to him and a cat on the other side of her to purr when
she stroked her. But Grandmother did not care for
animals.

"Always barking and gobbling up food," she said
when Eliza spoke about a dog.

"But a cat then, Grandmother?" pleaded the little
girl.

"Always mewing on the wrong side of the door!"
exclaimed her grandmother. "You have Dickie, and
his song is worth all the dogs and cats in the world."

But canaries aren't easy to pet or to talk to, and
Eliza still dreamed of a dog and a cat to come and
sit with her.

One day Eliza was walking with her grandmother
along the road to visit a neighbor when they noticed
an arbor of boughs by the side of the path, making
a green woodland shelter. In front of it were a man

and a woman, both young, very dark-skinned, with
bright handkerchiefs tied about their heads and a
little dark-skinned child playing at their feet. On all
sides there were rugs spread on the bushes as though
for sale, and the curious thing was that many of the
rugs had animals on them.

"Good morning, worthy dame, and you, my pretty
child," the young woman called to them as though
she were singing. "Would you want to buy a fine
rug this morning?"

The two stopped, for Eliza's grandmother wanted
a new rug to lay before the hearth, and while she
fingered them all to see that they were thick and
well-made, the little girl played with the dark-skinned
child, who took a great fancy to the doll she carried.

Eliza was generous.

"You may have it," she said. "Some day perhaps
my grandmother will make me another one." And
she gave the doll a last kiss and put her in the other
child's arms.

The dark young mother had seen all this and
smiled a curiously sweet smile.

"Look, Stan," she said to her husband, "here is
one who shall have only our best rugs."

33

Soon afterwards the grandmother said, "Yes, I shall take a rug and Eliza may choose it if she pleases."

Eliza was sure what rug she liked best. There was one with a little gay dog on it, but as she moved towards it the young rug-maker shook her head.

"That wouldn't do, my pretty child," she said. "Tino is excitable. But how about Prince? He is old and kind." And she showed Eliza a rug which had been lying a little out of sight. It had a woolly, dark-brown dog on it with a red collar and brown eyes

which showed their whites a little, as though he were looking up to be patted.

"Oh, I love that rug!" said Eliza, and so it was rolled up and paid for and she and her grandmother went home instead of going visiting.

The rug was laid beside the hearth and much admired.

A day or two later Eliza came into the room alone. Her grandmother had gone to the near-by market to sell butter and had left Eliza home to feed the hens.

The little girl drew out a stool and sat down before the fire. Something moved at her elbow, and looking about, she saw a large woolly brown dog in a red collar, with eyes rolled towards her as though he were waiting to be patted.

He was the most comfortable dog to pat. For more than an hour he played with Eliza, and then, when the grandmother came home, there he was in the rug again.

After that, whenever Eliza was alone, Prince appeared, ready to play or be patted, or just to sit near at hand for company. And whenever the grandmother was in the house, Prince was in the rug, and he never barked and he never gobbled up anything.

Eliza's grandmother wondered a little when Eliza took all the money out of her bank, which she had earned from the eggs of her own hens, and asked if she might buy another rug. Eliza found the young couple and their child just ready to move, with their rugs packed on the backs of two gray donkeys.

"Ah, here is the child who gave the doll," cried the young woman. "Stop the donkeys, Stan. If she wants another rug, she shall have another of our best. So it's a cat this time, is it, my pretty young lady? Here is a kitten which is as gentle as she is gay, and will suit Prince and you both."

So Eliza paid her money, and the rug was rolled up and put under her arm, and the strangers went on their way, leaving their withered bower behind them. And, after that, whenever Eliza was alone, she had two playmates, and this new one never mewed on the wrong side of the door, either. And when one day Eliza told her grandmother the secret, her grandmother was very pleased.

"Now, that's what I call sensible," she remarked. "You wanted pets, Eliza, and I wanted rugs. And it seems we both have what we want and no harm done. It took a clever woman to hook those rugs, my dear!"

SOMEONE
IS WAITING

Alas! at the window
Nearest the door
Someone's been waiting
An hour or more,
His nose at the pane
And his feet on the floor.

Someone is waiting,
Someone who knows
School must be out,
Someone who goes
To watch with his eyes
And to sniff with his nose.

"Where are the children?
Where can they be?
It's after two!
It's nearly three!
Have the children gone off
And forgotten ME?"

36

REGGIE

ONCE UPON A TIME there were a man and and woman who had a dog named Reggie. He liked the man and woman, and they liked him. They gave him a barrel with some straw in it to live in, and plenty of food and affection. Reggie was happy. Or very nearly happy. He liked everything about his new home except the barrel.

Reggie's barrel was a good barrel. It was painted red, and it kept out the rain and it was fixed so that it didn't roll when he got in and out of it. But all the other dogs in his neighborhood lived in dog houses and they laughed at him.

"Hi! Reggie!" they'd call as they went by. "How's your barrel?"

One day the man decided to build a garage which he and his wife thought they needed. He had cement brought for foundations and a lot of lumber and some windows, and he even bought paint to paint it when it was finished. He was a good man with his hands and every sunny day Reggie sat and watched him at work.

One day the man went in as usual to have lunch and when he came out again to work on his garage he couldn't find his hammer.

He went into the kitchen and said to his wife, "Have you seen my hammer?"

But his wife said, "No, dear. You must have mislaid it. I'll come out and help you look."

But though she looked and looked and he looked and looked they couldn't find the hammer.

So the man went to a neighbor's house and borrowed a hammer, but a minute later he was back in the kitchen.

"You haven't seen a box of nails anywhere, have you?" he asked his wife.

But his wife said, "No, dear. I'll come out and help you look."

But though she looked and looked and he looked and looked they couldn't find the nails.

And at last the man went to another neighbor to borrow some nails.

Well, all afternoon the same sort of thing happened.

The man couldn't find his saw and his wife couldn't either. And the man couldn't find an extra light of glass he was sure he had stood up against the side of the porch, and he couldn't find some of his paint and brushes, nor some of his boards and shingles, and his wife couldn't find them either.

So the man kept hunting and borrowing and working as he could, and by suppertime he was tired and ready to rest.

"I can't understand it," he said to his wife. "There's

37

been no one in this yard all day but ourselves and Reggie. Where have all those things disappeared to, and why, I ask you?"

His wife said, "Have some more potatoes and gravy, dear. Yes, it is very strange. But I suppose while we were having lunch someone came in and stole them all. Such things do happen."

"It must be that," said the man. "But there's something queer about it all. Why didn't Reggie bark? Tell me that."

"I can't," said his wife. "It *is* very strange."

"I've lost most of my afternoon's work," said the man. "And I'm tired out hunting for things which weren't there. I'm going to bed early."

"I feel tired, too," said his wife, "and it's a pity, for tonight there's to be a full moon and I thought we might go for a drive."

"If there were ten full moons, I'd still fall asleep," said the man.

So the man and the woman went to bed early and fell fast asleep and pretty soon the full moon rose and all the world was nearly as light as day.

Suddenly the man woke up and exclaimed, "Don't you hear a sound like sawing?"

His wife was still half asleep. "You were dreaming," she said, and they both went to sleep once more.

But a little later the man woke up and asked, "Don't you hear a sound like hammering?"

His wife opened one eye. "You were dreaming,"

she said, and they both went to sleep once more.

Very early in the morning the man woke again. The full moon must have been setting and the first light of dawn paled the east.

"Don't you hear a sound like a wet brush on boards?" he asked, but his wife scarcely woke up at all to answer.

"Dreaming," she said, but she was still in a dream herself, and the man yawned and went to sleep again.

In the morning when the man and his wife got up, everything seemed quite as usual. There was no sound of anything in the air, but the woman said, "I smell paint."

The man couldn't smell it.

"Maybe I left a paint pot uncovered," he said.

At breakfast time Reggie appeared at the screen door and ate his breakfast as usual. But he kept looking at the man and woman excitedly and wagging his tail. Then he'd run towards the door and look back to see if they had noticed him. At last he began to bark, and when no one paid any attention, he came and pulled at the man's trouser leg.

"He wants something," said the man. "You wait, Reggie, until we're through breakfast."

So Reggie waited, his ears pricked, his eyes shining, and his long, strong tail beating on the floor. It seemed a long time before the man and the woman were ready, but at last they said, "All right, boy. You show us."

Reggie jumped up, and when the door was opened, dashed out, barking and capering with joy. The man and the woman followed. Around the corner of the house they followed.

There stood the apple tree with the barrel under it, half in and half out of the shade.

But what was that *beside* the barrel?

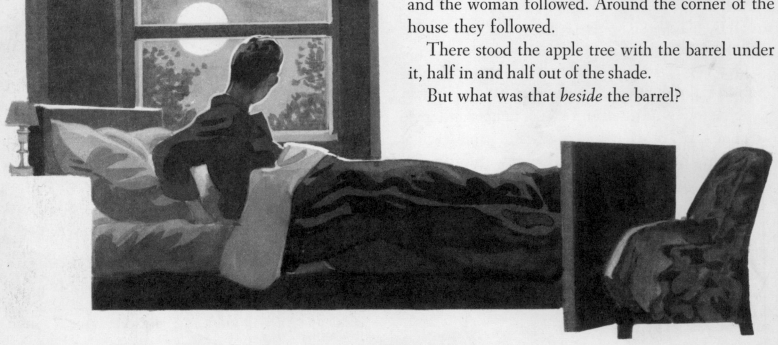

38

My goodness gracious mercy me! There stood a
beautiful white dog house with a neatly shingled roof,
and a little window on one side, and on the grass lay
the hammer and saw and the left-overs of boards and
a box of nails nearly empty, and a tin of paint with
the brush still in it.

And there was Reggie barking with joy and trying
to call their attention to the sign over the door which
had "Reggie" written on it in fresh paint, still shining wet.

For a while the man and woman just stood there,
staring.

Then at last the man said, "He's been watching me
at work for days."

The woman nodded.

"I guess he didn't like the barrel."

The man turned to Reggie. "You're a mighty smart
dog," he said.

"Isn't he?" asked the woman.

Reggie barked with joy. But their praise didn't
surprise him. He agreed with them.

39

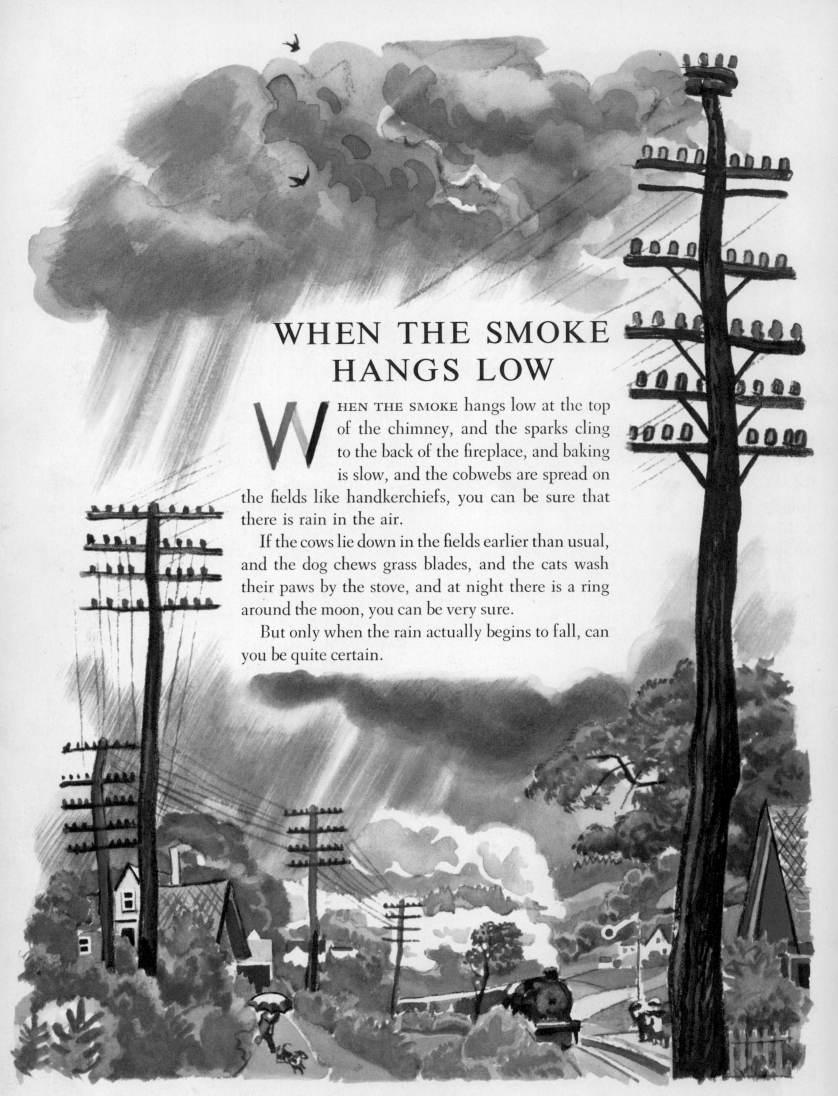

WHEN THE SMOKE HANGS LOW

WHEN THE SMOKE hangs low at the top of the chimney, and the sparks cling to the back of the fireplace, and baking is slow, and the cobwebs are spread on the fields like handkerchiefs, you can be sure that there is rain in the air.

If the cows lie down in the fields earlier than usual, and the dog chews grass blades, and the cats wash their paws by the stove, and at night there is a ring around the moon, you can be very sure.

But only when the rain actually begins to fall, can you be quite certain.

PRINCE CHARLIE

From where Jock Cameron and his sister Jeanie sat under the big pine tree beyond the lower oat field, they could see most of their father's farm and could watch their mother near the house as she hung out the clothes on the line. Below lay the hazy blue of the sea off the coast of Nova Scotia, and small in the distance there were a couple of sword-fishing boats, with a man high up on each masthead, on the lookout for the great fish for which they were cruising.

"We ought to stop eating blueberries or there won't be enough left for a pie," said Jeanie, at the same minute taking another handful from the basket between them.

"We'll pick some more before we go back," said Jock comfortably, helping himself.

Just then they heard old man Dalhousie shout, "Get out of here, you slinking tyke!" but they paid little attention. Old man Dalhousie, who owned the next farm, was always shouting at things. Jock and Jeanie went on eating berries, their red mouths turned blue.

Suddenly something moved in the yellow oats near them, and a little dog appeared, wagging his tail and cringing close to the ground, as though begging the children not to be cross with him. He was a dirty, shaggy little dog with cocked ears and frightened eyes.

"Mr. Dalhousie was driving him off," said Jeanie. "He must be a tramp dog. Ought we to drive him away, Jock?"

"Why should we?" said Jock. "Come here, boy. That's a good dog. Good dog." But as he reached out his hand to pat the small head, the dog dodged away.

"The poor little thing!" cried Jeanie, suddenly indignant. "Here, I have half a cooky left in my pocket. Come, dog, come, dog, here's something to eat."

The dog crept closer to her, and at last took the pieces of cooky, very gently, looking up each time to see if she were going to scold him. After a while he let the children pat him. As Jock rubbed his ears he gave him a little push and suddenly the stranger rushed off in a circle, barking, and ran back, his eyes dancing.

"He's trying to play," said Jock, but just as suddenly, the little dog became timid again, as though afraid that he had been too daring.

"He's very thin," said Jeanie. "Do you suppose Mother'd give him some bread and milk?"

"She might, but wait a minute."

Jeanie was silent while Jock thought.

"We'd better name him first, before we take him down," he said, after a little.

"Why?"

"Oh, because. A name makes him more real. Maybe we could keep him."

41

"But Father's going to get us a collie."

"Wouldn't you rather have this one?"

"Yes, I would," said Jeanie. "I'd rather have this one that came to us than any old bought collie in the world."

"Then we must name him."

"Rags?"

"No, Rags won't do. We don't want them to think of him as a tramp."

"Cooky? He's almost the color of the cooky I gave him."

"No, he needs a proud name to keep up his heart. We'll call him Prince Charlie."

Mrs. Cameron was a kindhearted woman, although severe.

"I'd never refuse a hungry creature food," she told the children, "but that broken-spirited mongrel's no sort of dog at all. The best thing will be for your father to shoot him, when he comes home. No, we'll not discuss it now. Talk to your father. But I've told you what I think."

Jock and Jeanie sat on each side of Prince Charlie, watching him eat. The little dog was so hungry, yet every once in a while he broke off eating to look up at them in a surprised, grateful sort of way.

Even their mother was touched.

"He seems a good little dog," she said, "but you can't keep him. You know your father's promised you a fine collie."

When Mr. Cameron came home with the horses from cutting the upper oat field, he saw Prince Charlie and shook his head.

"That's the dog belonged to one of the wood-cutters along the road," he said. "The man's shack burned down last week while he was away. He'd left the dog inside, with the stove going, and got back from town to find his place in flames. He got the dog out, but he doesn't seem to have cared much for him, because he left him behind when he took a job at Cape North. His hair's burned; that's what makes his coat so ragged. He'd look better when it grew out. But he's not worth keeping. No one ever got any good from a cur. What we want here is a purebred dog like the one I'm going to get, next time I drive to Sydney."

Jock wasn't accustomed to argue with his father. His face turned very red.

"We like Prince Charlie fine, sir, the both of us."

"We like him fine, Father," Jeanie joined in loyally. "He's a good little dog."

"He tried to play with us, Father, when he saw we wouldn't hurt him."

"The fine collie will have many friends, but we're the only ones to love little Prince Charlie."

"We might keep him a bit and see how he turns out," suggested the mother, from the stove.

The children gave her a grateful look. Here was help they hadn't dared count on.

Emboldened, Jeanie suddenly lifted Prince Charlie in her arms and carried him to her father.

"You hold him," she said. "He weighs no more than a rabbit. And the bones! But he's lapping your hand, Dad. He's a good little dog."

Mr. Cameron put Prince Charlie down on the ground. He said slowly, "You'd rather have this scared-of-his-shadow tyke than a fine purebred collie, you two? Think before you answer. This dog will never be a credit to you or to anyone else. Give me a sensible answer now, and say you'll take the collie."

Jock's blue eyes met his father's blue eyes.

"I'd rather have Prince Charlie, sir."

"Than a hundred collies!" cried Jeanie.

"Very well, then we'll say no more. You may keep the dog."

But Mr. Cameron's mouth looked stern and he scarcely spoke that evening at the table.

And so Prince Charlie's new life began. He was bathed in the brook with Mrs. Cameron's laundry soap until his stiff brush of hair was clean and as smooth as it could be made. He was fed until he forgot hunger, and played with until he forgot fear. Mrs. Cameron became nearly as fond of him as Jock and Jeanie were, but Mr. Cameron could not forgive Prince Charlie for not being a purebred collie. He never raised his voice to him, but he never patted him either, nor paid the slightest attention to him.

The days went on and Prince Charlie had become a pretty little dog, people said, when he went with the children to the store.

"He's a sort of terrier, maybe," Mr. Urquhart, who kept the store, suggested. "Now his coat's grown out, he's not so bad-looking."

"He has Dinmont blood in him," claimed lame Sandy Macpherson, who had bought half a pound of sugar an hour before and was standing about to hear the news before going home. "I have an old collar now on the kitchen shelf would just about fit Prince Charlie."

Even old Mr. Dalhousie stopped to pat Prince Charlie when they met on the road. Everyone had a kind word for him but the master of the house, and the shadow of Mr. Cameron's disapproval darkened the children's joy.

Winter came and Prince Charlie was allowed to sleep behind the kitchen stove. Very late one night Mr. Cameron was wakened by loud barking.

"Keep still there!" he shouted angrily, but instead of keeping still, Prince Charlie ran up the stairs and down the hall and into his room, all the time uttering shrill quick barks.

Mr. Cameron, half asleep and angered by the commotion, reached out of bed and flung his heavy shoe at the dog. There was a yelp, but instead of running away, Prince Charlie jumped straight onto the bed, barking still in the same high excited fashion.

"Have you gone mad?" Mr. Cameron asked furiously, flinging the dog to the floor. But the barking never stopped.

It was then that at last Mr. Cameron became wide-awake and smelled wood smoke in the air. Racing Prince Charlie to the kitchen, he found that the stove pipe had fallen, and that the floor was charring. A bucket or two of water stopped the danger in its beginnings. Mrs. Cameron, in her wrapper, stood whitefaced in the doorway, but Jock and Jeanie had not even wakened.

Mr. Cameron wiped his hands dry on the roller towel and picked up Prince Charlie, who had stopped barking.

"So you remembered what fire meant and came to wake me up?" Mr. Cameron asked in a voice he had never used to Prince Charlie before. "You're a dog with wits and I'm proud of you. We'll forget the past; is that agreed? Well, then, your bed's soaking wet, so you'd better come finish the night on mine. And I wouldn't be surprised if Jock and Jeanie will be pleased to find you there in the morning."

44

HE PRINCESS
AND THE NUTSHELL

It was a little nutshell,
A walnut shell,
A light shell.
The princess took it in her hand
And felt the small shell stir.
Surprised, she opened up the shell,
She fingered it,
She opened it,
And there a little greyhound stood
That barked and looked at her.

It was the smallest animal,
The prettiest,
The daintiest,
That anyone in all the court,—
In all the world—had seen.
The princess cried aloud with joy,
She danced
And sang aloud with joy,
And then she ran, all rosy-cheeked,
To show it to the queen.

45

THE TAIL-END THERE

When you are happy,
Bos'n, please,
Keep your tail away
From my poor knees.

Put your head-end here,
And your tail-end there,
And then you will only
Thrash the thin air.

TRIO

The little boy walked,
And on either side,
Stalking,
Walking,

Moving with pride,
The police dogs went,

Sharp nose, long tail,
Like wolves,
Good wolves,
In a fairy tale.

THE LITTLE DOG
OF THE MANCHU PRINCESS OF MU

THE LITTLE DOG of the Manchu Princess of Mu was a very proud little dog.

"I am the dog of the Manchu Princess of Mu," he told the cranes in the palace pool, and they bowed very politely, like thin old gentlemen wearing red skull caps.

"I am the dog of the Manchu Princess of Mu," he told the doves in the palace trees, and they all murmured dreamily, "Mu, Mu, Manchu Princess of Mu," until the leaves stirred softly with the sound.

"I am the dog of the Manchu Princess of Mu," he told the deer in the park, and they looked at him with wondering eyes, for in the forest where they had been born they had belonged to nobody.

"I am the dog of the Manchu Princess of Mu," he told the Emperor's monkey, who was tied by a silver chain to a ring of jade about his middle. And the Emperor's monkey chattered and went on stripping the yellow skin from the banana which he held in his strange black hand, and grinned, but said nothing, for he had nothing to say.

Of course the dog told the other little palace dogs who he was, but they were just as proud as he was. Their noses were just as short, their eyes were as large, their coats were as silky and their tails were as plumed as his own. And they *all* belonged to Princesses, too. One belonged to the Princess of Tang, and another to the Princess of Sung, and another, who looked like a chrysanthemum, belonged to the Princess of Penang.

"No one pays enough attention to me," the little dog thought. "If I could only go out into the great world beyond the Imperial gates, the common dogs would be delighted to see a dog who belongs to the Manchu Princess of Mu."

So one day, when the great red Imperial gates had been opened for a palace palanquin carrying a nobleman of the court, the little dog saw his chance and slipped out between the legs of the guards and disappeared into the great city of Peking.

His ears were deafened by the noise. Where were the courtyards and pools and flowering fruit trees to which he was accustomed? Where were the flutes of jade and ivory, and the doves with whistles tied to their coral legs which made a music when they rose into the air?

Here the crowds jostled in the narrow streets. Everywhere there were sandals moving and voices shouting and bodies shoving and dust rising. No one noticed the little dog, but people stepped on him and kicked against him, and worse even than people, there were oxen, too, coming in from the country with loads of wood and grain, wearing twists of straw rope through their noses; and there were lines of camels from the desert, which looked as tall as mountains to the little dog; and there were horses with hard, quick-moving hoofs.

"I don't believe I want to tell anyone who I am," thought the little dog. "I'd better go back to the palace. I don't like the city after all."

But when he went back to the palace gates, they were closed. "I am the dog of the Manchu Princess of Mu!" the little dog barked, but the guards were talking together and none of them heard him.

"I shall have to wait until another palace palanquin enters," thought the little dog. But things weren't as easy as all that.

Just then two ragged boys noticed him.

"Here's our chance!" shouted one. "The rag man will give us a copper for his skin."

And without more ado, the two boys began to chase the little dog.

How he ran, how he dodged, how he bit one of them in the ankle when he was cornered, how he hid, how he panted, how he ran on again, and how he at last escaped from them, I have no time to tell you here. But finally he left the boys behind.

How hot he was and how fast his heart beat! He had never been so thirsty in his life! But here there was no palace pool from which to drink. There was no saucer of food from which to eat. And worse still, in his flight, the little dog had gone so deeply into the city that among all the crooked streets and lanes he did not know how to find his way back to the palace.

At last he came to the market, and there he met a red rooster in a wicker basket. The rooster was almost his own color, a soft, bright red. He was the first small creature whom the little dog had seen, and besides that, he wasn't hurrying off anywhere. He was standing very still in his wicker basket.

The little dog stopped and tried to shake the dust from his coat. Then he said, as proudly as he could, "I am the dog of the Manchu Princess of Mu."

The rooster looked at him and his eye was bright and angry.

"You! you!" he exclaimed. "What are you but a dog? A hundred times I have chased a dog away from my flock at the Farm of the Southern Hills! It is I who am important! I shout, and the Sun comes! Morning after morning, I have proved this. Can you do that? Tell me, tell me, dog."

"Maybe not, but I am the dog of the Manchu Princess of Mu! And it seems to me that you are only a poor prisoner, Rooster."

"Certainly. And probably I shall die today. But tomorrow they will find out their mistake. For I am the Rooster who orders the Sun out of his roosting place! I know! I have proved it!"

And he gave a sharp peck at the little dog, which sent him hurrying on, hearing the rooster crow loudly behind him.

Next he came to a duck in a crate, but the duck was no more impressed by his announcement than the rooster had been. He was thinking of his canal, green as jade, under the willow trees, and cared not a feather for the dog or the Manchu Princess of Mu, either.

And then the little dog came to a goose tied by one leg and he told the goose who he was. But the goose would not listen. He was gabbling about the arrow of wild geese which had once flown over his master's farm.

"So high they were! So free! If I had only joined them, then, when I could! But I thought of the grain my master fed me, and the round hollow I had worn in the dust where I slept in the sun, and I lost my chance."

Then the little dog came to a cat, washing her paws in a doorway.

She at least showed no signs of ill-fortune, so he

gathered his courage for a last time to tell her politely
who he was.

After he had spoken, she glanced up, but her eye
was cold.

"Indeed? How interesting. Now in my case, my
master belongs to *me*. I chose him because he owns
a prosperous restaurant."

The little dog swallowed his pride.

"I am very hungry," he said.

"We never encourage beggars," replied the cat,
and went on washing her paw.

"Perhaps in this dark alley there may be food which
the cook has thrown out," the poor little dog thought,
and wearily he nosed his way into the littered lane
which ran beside the restaurant. But there were others
already there who had had the same thought.

As the little dog approached, three thin, big dogs
looked up from the meatless bones they were crack-
ing.

They looked at the little dog.

"Fat," remarked one.

"Juicy," remarked the second.

"Wait a minute," said the third. "Who are you,
stranger?"

In a small, small voice the little dog piped, "I am
the dog of the Manchu Princess of Mu."

The three dogs grinned and their teeth
looked long and sharp.

49

"Fat," repeated one.

"Juicy," repeated the other.

"Wait a minute," said the third. "Where do you live, stranger?"

"Behind the dragon wall," said the little dog, in a small, small voice.

"Fat," went on one.

"Juicy," went on the other.

"Wait a minute, you two. I have a fancy to see baby-face safely home. He's not big enough for a real meal anyhow."

"But he's fat," protested the first dog.

"He's juicy," protested the second.

"Go on with your bones," said the third, who seemed to be the leader. "As for you, Mu, come along with me."

So off went the little dog with his new companion and he was scared and dusty and hungry and thirsty and bewildered. Up one crowded lane they went and down another noisy one, in and out, in and out, with the big dog in front and the little dog behind, until at last they came to the rose-red dragon wall and the gates of the palace. And just then a palace palanquin arrived at the gates, and the attendants knocked and the guard opened to let in the great lord who wished to enter.

"Quick! Here's your chance!" exclaimed the big dog. "Yes! yes! I know! That's all right! In with you now!"

And before he knew it, the little dog had been hustled into the outer palace courtyard and the gates had clanged shut, and the big dog was gone.

How safe and happy the little dog felt to be home again! Never more did he venture to stick his little dark velvety nose out of the palace gates.

Everything was as it had always been. The cranes waded among the water lilies in the pools, the humming birds built their nests among the flowering trees, the crystal and jade ornaments of the Mandarins made a tinkling musical sound as they walked together, reciting poetry in the cool of the late afternoon.

Only now the little dog was different. For when the other little dogs boasted of the scented sleeves in which they were carried, the little dog was silent. But when at last the others asked him why he did not speak, he said:

"I have been out and have seen the great world, and in my wanderings, I have met a dog with a great heart. His only master was God. So now it seems a little matter not worth mentioning that I belong to the Manchu Princess of Mu."

WOLF DREAMS

The old dog slept
And the old dog dreamed,
Not of the carpet
On which he lay,
Not of the streets,
Not of the town,
Nor the house, nor the people,
He knew by day.

The old dog slept
And the old dog dreamed,
Dreamed of a forest
Deep and dark,
And of comrades who ran
By his running side,
Comrades who howled
But could not bark.

The deer is up,
The deer is in flight,
And the swift pack follows
Through forests deep,
And the old dog whimpers,
The old dog stirs,
And his feet are running
In his sleep.

51

NOW IN NOVEMBER

OW IN NOVEMBER, now in November, we waken to find the fields white and tousled like a rough-coated dog. There is a shine on the grasses if the sun comes out. Some day soon the windows will be furred with frost and we will peer out between the fronds of great ice ferns.

THE HUNTER

All night long
Across the sky
Orion the hunter
Goes striding by.

What is the quarry
He pursues
Through stars as bright
And thick as dews?

And who has heard
His great dog bark,
Sirius baying
Through the dark?

MAJOR AND MINOR

MAJOR WAS a fine young dog. He was as black as night, and strong and bold. His great-grandfather, the first Major, wore a collar of gold given to him by the passengers and crew of a vessel which had been wrecked off the coast of Newfoundland in such a gale that no boat could be put off from the shore to rescue them. But at the third attempt, Major the First succeeded in getting through the breakers and swimming out to the drowning men with a light line tied to his collar.

How he was dashed against the side of the vessel, and swept away again, and slammed down onto the slanting deck by one wave only to be washed off by another, before at last he half scrambled, half was pulled, to the upper part of the deck, and his precious line untied! Once the officers had that, they could haul a heavy line after it, and soon the heavy line was rigged between the shore and a mast of the vessel, and the women and the rest were being rescued in a breeches buoy pulled back and forth. The last to leave the ship was the captain; but the next to last was the big black Newfoundland dog who had saved them, taking his turn with the others.

So young Major had a fine ancestor to be proud of, and he was as brave and strong in the water as old Major had been. But somehow he was not a hero. There were no vessels to be rescued any more, and people got cross when he swam out to rescue them.

"Go away!" they shouted. "Will someone please call that dog? He's pulled me ashore twice and I'm sick of it!"

So when people were swimming, Major was usually shut up in the cottage and there he got into more

54

trouble. When he wagged his tail, ornaments flew off the low tables. When he pawed, chairs fell over. When he welcomed a newcomer, half the time he knocked him down.

"Major!" everyone shouted. "Go away!"

But if other people got cross with Major because he was young and clumsy and hadn't yet learned how to handle such big paws and such a long tail, there was one creature who actually hated him to the bottom of his heart. That creature was Minor, the little Chihuahua. Minor was as small as Major was large, a little elf of a dog beside a giant. Minor's feet were no bigger than five-cent pieces, and he moved as lightly as a dancer, and his bark was as shrill as the cry of a bird.

He growled and snapped every time the big, good-natured Major came near him.

And didn't he have good reason? The first time Major tried to play with the little dog, he put out his paw and Minor was knocked over and over and half crushed as well.

If Major took a lap or two at Minor's dish, the little dog's water or milk or dog food was gone in a moment, and Major was none the better for it.

If on a cool evening, Major lay down by the open fire, where was there any room left for Minor?

Oh, Minor hated Major and would never make friends. He sat on their mistress' lap and drew back his upper lip and snarled at Major when the big dog came anywhere near. He lay by their master's feet and bit Major in the leg if he dared to come up to be patted. And good, kind, black, clumsy Major looked surprised and unhappy and bumbled away, knocking something or other over as he went.

But one day, something happened. The family had already been bathing, and both dogs were allowed

out. Major lay on the beach, sleepily watching the waves breaking along the shore, and Minor followed their mistress onto the wharf. Minor was always very curious about things, so when he saw a crab in the fishing tin someone had left, he had to investigate. And before you could say Jack Robinson, the crab had him by the black tip of his nose, and Minor, backing away with a squeak, had fallen ten feet, smack, splash, into the sea!

The fall knocked the little dog's breath out of his body and before he could recover, he had taken a great swallow of sea water. His tiny paws beat helplessly as he went under. His master, talking to a friend on the beach, noticed nothing. His mistress, looking out to sea from the wharf, had no idea of what had happened.

But someone had seen. Major was on his feet and racing down the shore.

"Has that dog gone crazy?" his master, looking up, asked. "Come back here, Major! Come back, I say! Major!"

But Major did not hear. Already he was charging through the breakers, breasting the strength of the incoming seas. Now he was swimming as only a Newfoundland dog can swim, his black head surging forward with every dig of his strong paws.

"Where's Minor?" their mistress suddenly asked. "He was here a moment ago."

Then something moving in the water near the wharf caught her eye.

"Oh! oh!" she screamed. "He's fallen in! He's drowning! Help, someone! Help!"

But it was too late now for any human help from the beach or the wharf. The sea had the little dog and was pulling him under, and then loosening its hold for a moment, only to draw him down again. Minor was pawing wildly. In another moment it would be all over.

Just then, when hope was gone, something large and soft and curly rose up below the drowning Chihuahua and lifted him into the air, safely out of the water. Like a raft, Major swam under the little dog. If he had tried to take him in his jaws, Minor might still have drowned, but carried on those wide shoulders, he was as safe as in a boat, and in triumph he was brought to the shore.

From that day on, no one has ever scolded Major or called him clumsy.

"He is just like his great-grandfather, Major the First," everyone says, repeating the story of both rescues to anyone who will listen.

As for Minor, he scarcely leaves Major's side, and on warm days he sleeps in his shadow as in the shadow of a boulder, and on cold days, he sleeps between his paws close to the big dog's furry coat.

And whenever Major goes swimming, Minor goes swimming too. People stop whatever they are doing to watch them, thinking it a strange and pretty sight to see the big black dog far out beyond the breakers, with the little Chihuahua balanced on his shoulders, barking for joy.

For although he is not much of a swimmer, in his own way, Minor is as brave as Major, and now at last they are the best of friends.

THE CAST-IRON DOGS

N ALMIRA, a town in western New York, Judge Smith lived in a big brick house with stone steps leading down from the front door, and on either side of the steps there sat a cast-iron dog, as big and as black as a Newfoundland. All the children in town loved the big dogs. When they were very little, the children loved to pat them or make them collars of linked dandelion stems or daisy heads.

"When the big cast-iron dogs hear the firehouse bell ring, they bark," their fathers and mothers told the children.

So the children waited to hear the cast-iron dogs bark, but none waited as anxiously as a little boy named Andy Voss. No matter what he was doing,

when Andy heard the fire bells, he would jump up and race down the street for Judge Smith's house. But he was always too late to hear the cast-iron dogs bark.

One day Andy was cutting the side lawn at his house and the firehouse bells began to ring. Down went the lawn mower! Off went Andy! He ran faster than he had ever run before. And just before he turned the corner at Judge Smith's house, he heard a dog give a deep, low bark.

But when he reached the Judge's house, the dogs looked as they had always looked, sitting side by side with the walk between them and one cast-iron foot a little in front of the other, and their cast-iron eyes staring straight ahead of them.

"But I've heard you bark!" thought Andy Voss in

triumph. And when Mildred Denny at school said that a cast-iron dog couldn't hear the fire alarm and so would never bark, Andy replied loudly that he had heard one of them do it.

"That was the Irish setter at the Humbolts' next door," said Mildred.

"It was not!"

"It was, too!"

"It was not!"

And so the argument ran, until the bell rang for school and all the children clattered in to their desks.

Years went by and Judge Smith died and Mrs. Smith went to live with her daughter in another town, and the two cast-iron dogs were sold and taken away to an inn, where they were painted white with black spots and had baskets filled with artificial roses hanging from their mouths. The inn was called *The Dog and Basket Inn,* and Judge Smith's old cast-iron dogs went on gravely doing their duty in this new position. But here there were no children to make them real dandelion or daisy collars in the spring, and no one had ever been told that if they heard the fire alarm they would bark.

And pretty soon a newer inn had an even newer attraction in an elephant made out of driftwood, called *The Sea-Side Jumbo,* and fewer and fewer people came to *The Dog and Basket Inn,* until at last it was closed.

Andy Voss was grown up now, but he had never forgotten the cast-iron dogs, and when he heard that the inn was closing he called a meeting of the men of Almira.

"The town has been very dull these last years," he announced. "We can't tell our children to listen for the barking of the cast-iron dogs when they hear the fire alarm. There's no excitement; no one to make daisy chains for. We must bring the cast-iron dogs home, where they belong."

So an association was formed, and the dogs were bought for a great price—but what did money matter when it was a question of their own dogs?—and Mr. Andrew Voss with the help of young Andy and two neighbors and their children painted the dogs black again as they ought to be, and put them back where they belonged on either side of the stone steps. The people who live in Judge Smith's house are glad to have them there, but they don't own them. The dogs belong to the association and cannot be sold and cannot leave Almira.

And when a very little child begins to feel big, he reaches up and pats the noses of the cast-iron dogs, and when on a fine spring day little girls grow tired of playing with a ball on an elastic, they make a chain of big round dandelion links, or a daisy chain. And when the bell at the firehouse sounds the alarm, all the little boys run to hear the cast-iron dogs bark.

And it's funny, but of all the boys, it's only Andy Voss, Jr., who *thinks* he heard one of them, once. He's not quite sure, but he's almost sure. Yes, really, he's perfectly sure. And his father says he heard one bark, too. But only once.

THE DOG EXPLAINS

I HAVE to bark, said the dog, although of course I know that you're a neighbor and a friend of the family. But it is a promise that the first dog made to his master, and I keep the promise. Whenever I see a new face at the gate, whenever I hear an unexpected knock at the door, whenever a stranger's step sounds in the house, I must bark.

But I know you, and you can see by my tail that I'm really glad you have come. Do step in and have a visit with my people. Thanks to my barking, they'll be expecting you.

PUG ISLAND

 HERE ONCE WAS a little girl named Mary, who lived at the edge of a narrow lake, so narrow that she could see across to the house on the opposite shore where lived a fairy. Often she sat by her window or on a boulder by the shore and watched the charming things that went on outside the fairy's house. Most of all she loved to watch the scamperings and dancings of the fairy's little pug dog, an amusing creature with a cream-colored body and a round black head which looked as though he had poked his nose into a bowl of soot, and a tightly curled tail which was round as a doughnut.

More than anything else, Mary wanted a pug dog, and at last she got up her courage to go over to the fairy's house to ask her where one might be found.

She walked around the shore of the lake, and late in the morning arrived at the fairy's house. Everything was as pretty near by as it had seemed at a distance. She walked up the path bordered by flowers and rainbow-colored shells and knocked at the door, but it was not the fairy but the broom which opened the door for her.

The little girl looked at the broom in astonishment.

"Is the fairy at home?" she asked, when she could speak.

The broom handle shook from side to side, like a person shaking his head to say no. It was the pug dog which pattered forward and said pleasantly, "No, the mistress has gone to visit her aunt for a few days. Is there anything I can do for you?"

He beckoned her into the fairy's parlor, which was just as pretty as the garden had been, but Mary was a little surprised to find the broom sweeping all by itself, and a dustcloth flying about the air, wiping off the tops of the gay picture frames.

Before she could speak, however, a tray slid into the room with a glass of milk and some cookies on it, and a bowl of warm cereal and milk. It came to rest neatly on a little table by her chair, and the pug remarked, "The bowl of cereal is for me, so please put it on the floor. The rest is for you."

"But, but it all seems so queer," said the little girl.

"Doesn't your house know how to keep house for you?" the pug asked in surprise. "No, I suppose not. Fairies manage better than mortals. I suppose if I belonged to you, I shouldn't even be able to speak."

"I suppose not," said Mary.

They had finished their meal, and as she spoke the dishes hopped nimbly onto the tray, which sailed out into the kitchen, where Mary heard the hot water running and the dish mop mixing soap-suds in the sink.

"Well," said the pug, "can I help you, my dear?" Mary looked at him.

"You're just as charming here as you were from across the lake," she cried. "You see, I watch and watch and watch you, and I want a pug of my very own more than anything else in the world."

The pug looked pleased and jingled the bells on his collar, which immediately played *On the Bridge at Avignon.*

"There's nothing so hard about that," he said. "We'll just go over to the island and get one."

"Island?" asked Mary. "What island, Pug?"

"Pug Island," he replied. "Where the pug tree grows. Haven't you ever seen it?"

"I never knew there was an island in this lake," Mary replied, following the pug to the window.

As she started to look out, a spyglass obligingly winged through the air and fitted itself gently to her eye. Looking through it, sure enough she saw in the distance an island floating on the blue waters of the lake, and there seemed to be a tree upon it.

"Come along," said the pug.

The door flew open. The broom followed them politely to the steps. The duster waved in farewell. Mary and the pug ran out together and through the garden, across the lawn, down to the shore of the lake. There the pug blew a shrill whistle, and a boat appeared, rowed by four raccoons.

The little dog hopped in and Mary followed, the order was given for Pug Island, and the four raccoons rowed with a will. It seemed no time at all before the boat was beached and Mary was again following her guide.

In the middle of the island, rising from a lawn of green grass, was the tree Mary had seen. At first only its spreading shape caught Mary's eye, and then she saw that here and there among its leaves there was a cream-colored flower marked with black. But no! it was not a flower at all, but a small curled-up dog, asleep with its eyes shut, swaying a little on the long low branches.

Mary ran toward the nearest one, but the fairy's pug stopped her.

"Don't pick that one," he said. "Tail's not curly enough."

Mary turned, and seeing another sweet, round, wrinkled-up face, ran towards it.

"No!" cried the fairy's pug. "That one hasn't enough whiskers."

For some time he followed her about, giving her advice, until at last they came to a very small dog-flower with a particularly charming head.

"Yes, this one will do nicely," the fairy's pug said. "Pick it, my dear."

"Do I really pick it?" the child asked in wonder.

"Why, you always hear about people picking a dog!" said the fairy's pug, a little crossly. "Snap the stem, and then lay it in the grass until it wakes up."

Very carefully, Mary did as she was told. In a
few minutes the pug-puppy she had picked yawned,
stretched, and jumped up to its little feet. It seemed
to know immediately that it belonged to Mary, and
ran to her, jingling its three little bells and frisking
about her like a playful toy.

"Yours won't be able to talk, of course," said the
fairy's pug, "but you'll find it satisfactory, I'm sure."
And Mary has.

THE DOG HAS GONE HUNTING

The dog has gone hunting,
He's hunting for rabbits,
He chases them, baying,
He's full of bad habits!
No, he doesn't catch rabbits,
He's wild about chases,
He shouts to a rabbit
And then they run races.

The dog has come home,
He has drunk his dish dry,
Now he lies in the shade
But he's rolling his eye,
And he's thumping his tail
And he's waiting, because
He wants me to come
And take burrs from his paws.

NO ONE OWNS SANDY

O ONE owns Sandy. Sandy owns him-self, and perhaps he owns the town. Clementsville is not a large town; there are less than two thousand people in it, but there are a good many passers-by, since it is on a highway.

One day Sandy came to town. People said later that he came from the direction of St. Louis, but no one knows for certain. He didn't act like a lost dog. He trotted along the side of the road in a very self-pos-sessed fashion. He didn't have a collar, but he didn't seem dirty or hungry. He was a big, sandy-colored, short-haired dog, with a broad forehead and a narrow, light tan stripe down his chest. He had the strong, gentle look of a mastiff. Big as he was, no one has ever felt afraid of Sandy.

His first day at Clementsville, Sandy caused little comment. Mrs. Denny came out of her front door and found him lapping the milk from the cat's saucer.

She shouted and shook her apron at him, but Sandy looked up in such a friendly way, waving his big tail, that next minute she was bringing him a bone she had meant to use for soup. He stopped at the drugstore door that afternoon and pushed open the screen door. Dan Berry, behind the ice-cream counter, tried to drive him out, but Sandy just sat down, his big mouth open in a sort of smile, his lion-colored eyes smiling, and before he was through, Dan had to coax him out with a ten-cent cone of chocolate ice cream, and half a dozen of the kids shared theirs with him.

He got his supper from two taxicab drivers who

have a booth on the busiest corner of Clementsville where the St. Louis bus stops. Sandy sat down quietly beside them, watching them eat their sandwiches with alert good manners, until at last they invited him to join them.

"Well, so long, old fellow," one of them said later as he drove off. "Expect you'll be a good piece down the road by this time tomorrow."

But next day Sandy was not down the road. He was right here at Clementsville. Somehow he seemed to like the town. And here he has stayed. At first several people tried to take him home with them, but though he went politely enough he would not stay. One man even tied him with a rope, but Sandy quietly gnawed through it, and off he went to visit all his friends.

Slowly Sandy became known to every man, woman and child in Clementsville. He treated them all as his friends, and they treated him in the same way. He joined the children in the playground, he sat beside ladies waiting for the bus at the corner, he went to the Willow Lunch Room when he wanted to eat. He went to the drugstore when he wanted ice cream, he walked home with Pete Belknap, the grocer, when he shut up shop, he called on old Mrs. Sykes, who was sick in bed. He never chased cats, nor bit dogs, nor frightened children.

Sandy was the friend of all the town. You might find him anywhere, visiting with anyone, but his favorite place was the busiest corner, where the St. Louis bus stopped and the taxi men had their little office.

It was Bill Greene, one of the taxicab drivers, who suggested that Sandy had better have a house of his own, beside their building.

"And he ought to have a collar," said the other driver.

"Then there's a license," said Bill.

Just then the editor of the little weekly paper happened to pass by, and Bill Greene hailed him.

"Say, Mr. Kellogg, would you run an ad in your paper to raise a little money for Sandy?"

And they explained matters to Mr. Kellogg, while Sandy listened, looking as though he understood every word that was said.

Mr. Kellogg looked at Sandy over his glasses and nodded.

"I'll take care of that," he said. "I'll send Jim over to take some pictures and we'll start the Sandy Fund."

So next week there was half a column all about Sandy and what people had said about him, and Sandy's picture, smiling, was at the top. The money came rolling in. At the end of two weeks, the campaign was closed, and Mr. Kellogg and Bill Greene deposited forty-seven dollars and thirty-two cents in the Clementsville bank to the credit of Sandy, with themselves as trustees.

The first day Sandy drew out money for a good collar and his license to hang from it, and enough for lumber, paint, and nails for his house. But no one would let him pay for the collar or the license or the materials. The town clerk said that his case was exceptional, and the lumber yard and the hardware store donated the collar, paint, and nails, and Bill Greene and the other taxicab man built a fine large house with a sign on top that had Sandy's name on it.

Sandy has accepted this gift from the town and usually spends his nights in his own house, although once in a while he still prefers a friend's doormat. He continues to go where he pleases for his meals. One or two deep barks at any door is enough to have it opened to him, and in most houses there is a special dish put aside for Sandy. Everyone considers a visit from him as an honor.

He is always mascot when the home baseball team plays another team, and he leads the Fourth of July parade with a red, white and blue ribbon on his collar. He will keep an eye on a small child while the mother

hangs up the laundry, to see that it doesn't toddle off into the street. He will let little boys and girls ride on his back. He will lay his head on an old man's knee and quietly look up into his face. Nobody knows how the town got on before Sandy came. But now he is here and he gives no sign of ever intending to leave.

The only trouble is, Mr. Kellogg and Bill Greene and Sandy are worried about Sandy's bank account. He's tried to spend it, but no one ever lets him pay for anything. Sandy has about decided that as a dog with money, it's up to him to help less fortunate animals. I understand he paid the vet for setting a cat's leg the other day, and last week he helped a little boy buy his puppy a license. If you are in Clementsville and know of any other animal in trouble, just hunt up Sandy and his trustees.

THERE WAS A LITTLE DOG

There was a little dog,
Heigh ho, heigh ho,
And his body was long
And his legs were low,
And his coat was thin
And his eyes were bright,
And he went by himself
For a walk one night.

Now wouldn't you think,
Heigh ho, heigh ho,
That even a little
House-dog would know,
That it wasn't wise
And it wasn't good
To walk by himself
Alone in the wood?

Just what occurred,
Heigh ho, heigh ho,
Or whom he met
When the moon was low,
I cannot say,
For I might not be right:
But I do know that now
He stays home at night!

16 - 14 8 4